Say Nothing Saw W<

Joel Thomas Hynes

Say Nothing Saw Wood

JOEL THOMAS HYNES

Drawings by Gerald L. Squires

Author's Note

There was a violent murder in my hometown of Calvert (pop. 300) more than forty years ago. This is not that story. I want to be absolutely clear about that. I've lifted a few facts from newspaper clippings and court documents, otherwise the characters depicted in this little book are inventions of my imagination.

In some twisted, idealistic, and egocentric way, this is more my own story than anyone else's. I dont know how to explain that, except to recount a time when I was seventeen years old and not exactly living the good life — failing out of high school, waking up all too often in some jail cell, snapping to attention in some court room when I heard my name bawled out by another bloated judge, falling out with strangers, smashing things up, and destroying myself. Anyway, one bright summer morning I was stumbling along a narrow strip of pavement, on the outskirts of a small town near my own, bleeding from a cut above my eye. No idea how I'd gotten cut open, but I must have been bleeding for a while. Walking along like that, dazed and still mildly drunk, I idly scooped up a fist-sized rock off the side of the road. Not aiming at anything in particular, I let it drift up into the sky. Maybe I was tryna kill a seagull, I dont know. As soon as the rock left my hand a man walked out from a hidden driveway with two little girls, each holding one of his hands. I'd place them now at about two and three years old. Maybe. Hard to keep things straight. Time. I watched that chunk of rock climb into the air and arc down towards the man and his two little girls. It was headed directly for the little one on the outside. I felt my stomach turn, that crippling flash of adrenaline that originates in absolute terror. It would have killed her. Would have cracked her skull wide open and killed her. There was no one else around, no real reason for me to have thrown that rock. Given the state of my reputation at the time I wouldnt have had a leg to stand on in court or in the community. I would have been picked up by the cops, bleeding from my head and stinking like an abandoned brewery. I already had a hefty youth record at the time. I would have went to jail for a long time. And I would be remembered now for nothing else but being that saucy nuisance who killed a little girl with a rock. But the rock missed, of course. Barely. By inches, maybe. Neither the man or the girls noticed it when it hit the road alongside of them. I think about that morning every now and then and wonder why the wind wasnt different, why I didnt turn my body a different way, throw that rock a little harder, a little softer, why that little girl didnt tug at her father's arm at that last moment and step right into its path. Basically it astounds me sometimes that I was spared, that that little girl was spared, that family. I guess I find it daunting, and worth writing about, how randomly our fates are doled out. Because maybe the wind did pick up, maybe that little girl resisted the urge to tug at her father's arm for some reason. Maybe fate did intervene.

When I think back now on the wild, raging, self-destructive teenager I used to be, it's baffling not only that I eventually pulled myself up out of it, but that I made it out alive at all. It's the "what if" that tends to haunt us all, on some level, at some point in our lives, and certainly it became a driving theme for Jude Traynor, my narrator in *SNSW*. But to reiterate, Jude is a work of fiction. There is no romance, no passion, no mystery, no real logic at all to what happened in Calvert forty years ago. That one is a cold, ignorant, irredeemable story that's best left buried in the past.

— JTH

O' great saint Jude, whose traitor-sounding name, by man's perceptions crude, confused is with the infamy and blame of him who to our gain and his disaster betrayed so kind a Master.

Lost causes. Great St. Jude. Jude Shannon Traynor. Sounds a bit girlish I s'pose. Shannon is after me mother. Never knew her. Traynor being me father's crowd. Leonard J. Traynor, so says me birth certificate. J for Joseph or John, one of them other bible names. Use to think it mighta stood for Jude. Len's long gone too. All was left of him was the hood of his oilskin coat. Boat was called the *Shannon Marie*. People said Len was just askin for it to name 'er after a dead woman. I always thought it was a nice name for a boat.

They were takin in their gillnets for the year-end. Himself and his brother Angus. October. That undertow off Claire's Head. So. Yeah. Angus, every time he told the story he always told it different. Sometimes he said Len fell overboard and other times he said he jumped. They stuck the hood of Len's oilskin into a coffin with a set of rosary beads, a few flowers. Sunk the works into the dirt.

Dont remember much about Leonard. At the hay in the stable one summer, gettin me to jump it down. Never leave the prong lyin flat in the hay. Accident waitin to happen. I got one decent memory of his face, 'bout a month before he was lost. Maybe. Hard to keep things straight. Sometimes I dont know if a memory is a real thing or just some lie I'm tellin meself to help me get by.

Len, standin at me mother's grave. Sunday clothes. Hard time keepin his balance, sorta lopsided. He dont say a word. Blesses hisself, bangs a nail back into her fence with a chunk of marble. Turns and looks at me. I'm sure he's gonna crack me one. His teeth are… and his eyes. I used to like to think I had his eyes. Grabs me by the back of the neck and shoves me forward. I trips, lands face first onto me mother's grave. Next he got me up in his arms, walkin me out through the gates of the graveyard. Funny walk, like he got a limp in both legs. Thick smell of tobacco off him. Tobacco and salt fish.

Tomorrow's the fifteenth. Twelve years to the day I was shipped off to Dorchester. Life-seven. Non-capital murder. There's no such thing as that no more. All a matter of degrees nowadays. I aint been back to the Cove in twelve years. I s'pose I'm calmed down a bit. Jail. Few years workin the bush out west, after I got out. Cracked to be headed back, what? I mean, I shagged it up once. Once. I was seventeen years old. A lifetime ago. Sharp as yesterday sometimes too.

The night her purse was found I took to the woods behind the house. Sloshed me way through the Beaver Gullies till I hit the highway in back of the Cove. Long old night. Got a run though. Right to Town. Knocked around the bars on Water Street. Got talkin to some foreign fella off the boats. Offered me a berth. Vodka. I came to in Victoria Park, just about froze to the ground, some old queer rootin at me belt. Missed me boat of course. I got drunker then. Later on that morning I read me name in the paper. Jude Shannon Traynor. It was funny, seein it in print like that. I read it over and over. Just that bit. Just me name.

Couple more days beatin around Town like that and gettin picked up was a bit of a relief, really. Smell of diesel, me head bouncin off the steel floor of the paddy wagon. I started screamin for Margie. I mighta been bawlin.

"You need not say anything, you have nothing to hope from any promise or favour and nothing to fear from any threat, whether or not you say anything. Anything you say may be used as evidence."

Say nothing, saw wood, I said, over and over. Say nothing, saw wood.

Eight weeks locked up in St. John's waitin to go to court. Lawyers. Doctors. Mounties. Plead guilty, make it easier on yourself. Not guilty, I said. Well, they paraded every arsehole and his dog into the court to have a say about me. This head doctor makin me out to be some kinda crackpot. Fellas I hung around with all me life.

Margie. She wouldnt even look at me in the court. Never once came to see me all the while I was held in St. John's. Wrote her a bunch of letters from Dorchester. She never wrote back. They werent exactly love letters I s'pose. Couple of letters from Harold when I first went away. Deep shit, how some moose tried to mount a cow in the lower meadow. Harold. One thing that struck me as odd though was Harold's version of how the purse was found. How Mrs. Alfreda's horse found the purse in the stall of our stable, carried it down the lane in his mouth and dropped it at Angus's feet. But how there was a few fellas standing around at the time. Don Keough and them. How they all put it together that something wasnt quite right, that there mighta been something else. Poor old Angus, no choice but to turn me in. I s'pose it all gets twisted up after a while and it dont matter what the truth is so long as there's a good story. And everyone else's hands are clean.

Harold turned on me in the court too. People got no sense of loyalty no more.

Loyalty? Got word a while back that Angus had his head cracked open in a bar in St. John's. By some loyal business associate. Few and far between in Angus's trade. Never killed him, but might as well have, from what I can gather. Spoon-feedin him at the Waterford nowadays.

Uncle Angus. He packed it all in after Len was lost, sold the *Shannon Marie*. I went to live with him then. I was five. He sold weed, bit of liquor. Mounties'd turn the house bottom up, leave in a huff, never able to come up with so much as a seed. Angus shoutin about a warrant. When they were gone I'd scurry into me room to find me clothes and stuff scattered all over the floor. One time me mattress was sliced right down the middle. I just flipped it around the other way.

Then one day Angus aint home when the Mounties comes knockin. They barges right in. Lawlor, starts drillin me. Do you know where your father's gone? Do you know when your father'll be back? I says me father's dead. They nods, smirks down their noses, pokes around, scribbles in the book. I dont tell 'em nothing, cause I dont know nothing. Big black boots and hats. Guns. They're the Mounties. Say nothing saw wood.

Angus busts through the door then, full to the gills. Lunges at the cops. They each grabs an arm and he does a little spin, swings the two of 'em around the kitchen like he's dancin at the garden party with a couple of youngsters. The veins in his forehead. He never takes his eyes off me. But the Mounties, they're in top-notch shape and they got the height on Angus, so before I knows it they're loadin him into the back of their car and he's gone. Next morning I wakes up to the feel of his belt crackin across the side of me face. I keeps sayin I never done nothing! I never said nothing to 'em.

— This is just to make sure you never do.

Seven stitches over me eye. Swoll up, black and green for six weeks. Great big blue pills for the pain. Doctor down in Ferryland wants to know how it happened. None of your goddamn business, Angus says. Yeah, saw wood.

What else? I robbed a fair bit, eggs from henhouses and one time I even made off with Clar Hayden's hen. But I got caught for that and Angus nailed me.

— Not for stealin, for gettin caught.

The bottomless pit, Angus useta call me. Fish wasnt hard to come by. Turnips and carrots. Eat them raw. Plums and crabapples. Lotsa berries on the go. Winters though, I'd be half-starved. One time I ate a big greasy slab of butter. Spent three days heavin up. But hey, at least we had butter.

Christmas. I'm seven or eight. Not exactly waitin up for Sanny Claus. Someone leaves a canvas bag full of grub on our front step. A few books there too. Angus slung the works down the lane into the snow, cursin about the bigheaded whore who took him for a charity case. Sat down to the table with his bottle, talkin through his teeth at me:

— Poor little orphan. Held here against your will, are ya? Your own father couldnt stand the sight of ya. Threw himself overboard cause ya turned his goddamn guts! Why should I want ya?

I waited til he passed out 'fore I went down to find the bag. Bread and cream, chunk of boiled ham. Fruitcake tied up with a red ribbon. I never bothered with the books, but I gorged on that ham. Still eatin the cake well into the New Year. Never gave much thought to who mighta left the bag, but nowadays I got a pretty good idea.

Later on that year, August, Angus was locked up for breakin into a shop in Tors Cove. I was wondering where all the smokes come from. Mounties said he'd be gone for a long while. Told me to sit tight till someone came back to figure out where I was gonna go. Angus, laughin when they led him down the path in handcuffs.

— Run for the hills Judy! They knows about the hen too!

He was always pumpin me full of stories about the orphanage in St. John's.

— Your rightful home.

I belted 'er up through the woods towards Claire's Head. You can see the whole harbour from the Head. I watched the Mountie's car coast down the South Side towards Ferryland. And waited.

I got hungry. Afraid to go back down to the house. Filled up on crabapples that were nowhere near ripe. Dozed for a bit under the tree. Woke up a while later with an odd feeling that I was being looked at. Watched.

Then out of the woods walked Mrs. Alfreda Jacks.

I'd never seen her up close like this. Dont go up near the woods on the Head cause Alfreda Jacks might…I dont know…boil you up or skin you or something.

Long, tangly grey hair. All mops and brooms, like they says. Big bucket of squashberries in her hand. Her shadow across me legs. She scanned the ground around me. Near on two dozen little apple cores scattered about. Shook her head.

— Mind now, the state of your belly, time them green apples does their work.

She barely had the words out 'fore I curled up with a brutal cramp in the guts.

— Come on then, see if we cant set you straight.

Alfreda Jacks. Her name whispered and swore on for as long as I could remember. If your greens werent comin up full, then Alfreda Jacks must have put a… a curse or something on it. Stories about a little girl lost in around her place years ago. Dont let her look you straight in the eye. That sort of talk. But if your horse took sick she was the first to be sent for. People were odd like that about her. Alfreda Jacks. Standin in front of me with her hand out, lookin to lead me off through the woods. Another cramp shot through me guts. The sun was going down. I had nowhere else to go.

But her house was only normal. Lots of knittin around. Bread dough. Dark old wood chairs. Smell of kerosene. Candles and lamps everywhere. She had an old flag out front, flappin at half-mast. When I got me nerve up and asked her about it she says to me:

— There's always someone dead or dyin somewhere Jude.

She gave me a dose of baking soda and some minty stuff. Straightened me guts out. And… I stayed on with her for well into the fall. Mid October. She was always riggin up the wicked grub.

Sat me down to me letters and I actually got 'em in me head. I mean, they tried to teach that stuff in the school but I always found it a useless jumble.

Mountie showed up one evening. I hid in the back room. Lawlor, nosing about. Tryna hint that maybe I was too much for her to handle on her own. She laughed at that. Then she's says to Lawlor, she says:

— He's welcome here so long as he wants to stay.

I barely left her side after that. Trudgin down along the cliffs and the groves with her. Leaves and berries and roots. Jesus, she had a use for everything. She had snares out too. First time ever I was at that. Some dirty, skinnin rabbits. Some stink.

She had a horse. Sal. She'd give a whistle and right away he'd come trottin to her, nuzzle into her. I never could get the whistle right. I'd seen him before, down on the road or grazin up in the meadow. Never knew it was her horse.

So I knocked around with Mrs. Alfreda like that for a while. We got on good, things were alright. And then Angus was let out and I had to go home out of it.

He came poundin on her door one morning, barkin out me name. I was half asleep. Dandy big down-filled quilts Mrs. Alfreda had. She asked him to come in. She called him Mr. Traynor. He stood out on the doorstep, cursin at her.

— Jude love, come down. Your uncle's here for ya.

Sometimes I thinks if he'd never come for me that day, wiped his hands clean of me, then maybe things mighta…

Of course I was up to Mrs. Alfreda's every chance I got. He'd go off on a tear and she kept me fed while he was gone. I did lots of work for her: mendin fences, cleanin out the henhouse, at the wood. And like I said she had me sat down to me letters and numbers and such. But she never got on me case about sayin prayers or bible stuff. Her husband was thirty years dead. Something about the way he died that turned her from prayers.

She had lotsa books though. Charles Dickens and what's-his-face, the Russian fella. Meself, I'd never seen the sense, starin into a book for an hour. But when she'd read to me, the lamp flickerin off the walls and her eyes racin across the pages, I dont know, it was something else. And she'd always ask me questions about it, what I thought about what this character said or how do I think this fella might get outta this situation. *David Copperfield.* I re-read that one in jail. *Cannery Row*, that was a funny one, the b'ys were cracked in that. *Treasure Island.* And that Poe fella, he used ta frighten the shit outta me. Some evenings, after she'd read me that stuff, I'd have to get her to walk me back down to the edge of her land till we could see the lights from Angus's place. Then I'd take off, flat out in the dark. I always useta dream about that, tearin through the dark, no real destination but tryna outrun whatever's comin behind me, heart poundin, shadows grabbin for me ankles, hookin their claws into me arms and shoulders. Never a bad dream. Just the sense that what was at the end of the line was that much darker than what was comin behind me anyhow. I'd always wake up soon as I hit the back porch of our house.

    Home.

I learned to step around Angus, when not to look at him. If he wasnt laced out of his head he was comin down and spoilin for a brawl. I done something one day, pissed him off, and he held a chisel to me throat. I told Mrs. Alfreda about it. She never said a word. But she dropped a bit of a bomb on me later on. Only a little nip of the whole story. Just a taste.

    We're checkin our snares in back of the grove. We got a rabbit and a grouse right off the bat. Both in my snares. This last one I was after settin up, dandy little rabbit path, in off the main track. When we comes to the marker I drops down to me belly and looks in at the snare. Sure enough. Not a rabbit though. Or a grouse. Fox. Big fella, pale orange with a streak of white stretchin underneath from his neck to his tail. Caught be the hind leg. Three or four snares looped around his neck. He musta been followin the one scent and just busted right through 'em all. No way he's gettin out of it though. The snare tight around his back leg. He keeps tryna step back through it.

Mrs. Alfreda hands me the axe.

— Here. You'll have to tap 'im with this.

Why, I dont know. Seems to me if we cant eat 'im we might as well let 'im go. She says, you let 'im go and he'll turn on ya. And if we leaves 'im he'll only chew his leg off and die anyhow.

I'd seen her before, killin a rabbit when it was still kickin in the snare. I crawls in on me belly, the fox snarlin and growlin at me. His hind leg matted with blood. When I gets near enough and able to kneel up a bit he starts barkin at me. Just like any old mutt you'd see on side of the road. I tries talkin to 'im then. Hey buddy, here little fella, I says. Alfreda says knock it off, just get it done. She's lyin flat in the moss, lookin in on us. I edges closer to the fox. Sure enough then, he goes for his back leg, shallow little nips at first, but then he rips a tuft of fur clear off the leg. And he yelps when he does that, but goes right back at it. Gnawin at the raw, bubbly flesh underneath. I raises the hatchet.

— Jesus Jude not that way, turn it around b'y. He'll be no good for stuffin.

I turns the head of the hatchet around, so the blade is facin me. But I feels something. Some flicker. That maybe it's gutless and weak of me, what I'm about to do. That if I really wants him to live I can just risk it and cut the snare free. He might just run. I knows I would. But there's something else in me too, something that wants to consume some part of him I cant see, own the light in his eyes, breathe his last breath. Or, I dont know, maybe just to see what would happen.

He makes another snarl at me. I dont budge. No fear in me. Just calm. It's for his own good. He goes back to gnawin at his leg. I strikes him, hard as I can, right in the centre of his skull. He falls. Mrs. Alfreda's hand gripped around me ankle, ready to yank me back out to the track, just in case. But I knows he's dead. It's instant. I can feel him die. The *sound* of his death, the hollow pop. I lifts his front paw and lays me hand where I figures his heart should be. Nothing. Soft and warm.

I cuts the snare free, drags him out to the track and lays 'im at her feet. She picks 'im up by the tail, gives 'im a twirl and slings 'im over her shoulder. She said it was the first fox she laid eyes on in them woods in over twenty years.

— You done good Jude, you done good.

She put her arm around me on the way out. I leant into her, let her carry me along like that. The sun was going down and the woods were right quiet. I done good.

Time we got down to her house the back of her jacket was drenched in blood where the fox bled out of his mouth. She hung all three catches from a beam in the stable and we went inside. Said she was gonna stuff the fox herself. She said then, how me mother used to love a feed of rabbit. And of course I latched onto that and started askin all kinds of questions, wantin to know how she died and how old was I when she did. Mrs. Alfreda went straight for the kettle, slumped down in her chair with her tea when it was ready. But she told. Not all of it, not then, but she told me enough:

The night I was born, big snowstorm. And my mother never made it. She was too small. Mrs. Alfreda hadda cut her open. To save me. It woulda killed us both, no doubt. No phone. Roads werent fit for an ambulance. She hadda cut her. Slipped me out and did her best to patch me mother up. And Len was there. And Angus. Mrs. Alfreda said they got into it, had a big brawl. She wouldnt tell me what about, on the night I was born, while me mother lay dyin. She wouldnt say.

She brought down an old hatbox from a cupboard above the

stove. I watched her fuss around in it. She pulled out a gold chain with a fancy little round watch on it.

— Belonged to your mother, she said.

I asked her could I have it. She said when I was old enough, when I was ready, then she'd let me have it. I stared at it, swayin back and forth like in her hand. The fox's blood caked black under her fingernails. She laid a little brown envelope on the table. I thought I saw the corner of a twenty pokin out. She caught me lookin then, buried the envelope deeper into the box. Finally she handed me a dented old metal flask. She said he'd dropped it at her house the night I was born. During the scuffle. A name was engraved on it: *Traynor, Leonard J., First Mate.* The other side said *The Lady Margaret, 1954.*

Cargo boat outta Nova Scotia. There was another lad from up the Shore on board too. Fella with one arm, a real nuisance, she said. Headed for St. John's and went down off Cape Race. No one lost.

— That's the night poor Leonard had his accident, she said.

— What accident? I asked right quick.

But she stopped, like she'd said more'n she wanted to. I hounded her to fill in the blanks. She wouldnt.

Lyin in bed that night with the scent of the fox on me hands. The smell of its death. And Alfreda, talkin to me like that, like I was

a friend, someone to be trusted. I felt this…shift. I sat up and looked at me reflection in the glass of me bedroom window. It was like I was seeing… well I didnt know what to make of what I saw. I got up and filled the washbowl. Couldnt sleep with the smell of that fox on me hands. I scrubbed and scrubbed but I could smell it for weeks after. I can pretty much smell it now.

Later on that year I got me first piece of tail. Teresa Bennett. Meself and Harold were jiggin sea trout down off the breakwater when she come trudgin across the beach. Sixteen, I s'pose she was. Heavy too. She used to call me the lost cause.
   — Here comes the little lost cause.
   Big manly roars out of her then. It was years later that I figured out she was just pokin fun at me name. And by that time she was dead. Loaded drunk, fell out the back of a truck near Bay Bulls somewhere. All of a sudden then everyone loved her.
   That day on the beach she up and started tossin rocks and chunks of driftwood out at our lines. Lookin to piss someone off. Harold called her an old slut and fired a rock at her. She fired one back, a big one, caught me right in the corner of the goddamn eye. An inch closer and I'da been the real hard ticket, right out of the movies, with the black eye-patch and the empty socket to show

around at the dances. Blood streamin down me face. I picked up
a handful of rocks and let drift at her. She took off back up the
beach and I took off after her. She was fast too, for the size of her.
I kept drillin rocks at her while I was runnin and she was screamin
back at me that she was sorry, that it was an accident. I was half
blind with the blood runnin into me eyes. She lumbered up the
bank and busted into the Reddys' old stage. Time I got to the door
she had it barred off. I could hear her trying to steady her lungs.
I kept heavin me shoulder into the door until I broke one of the
boards. I gave it one last go at exactly the same time she got out of
the way. I landed in on the floor then, and drove a fuck of a nail into
me hand. That hurt worse than the rock in the face. She took off to
the other end of the stage but the backdoor was boarded up. I had
her cornered. And I realized then that I'd no clue what I was plannin
to do with her when I caught her. I was just chasin her cause I was
cracked. But then, when I seen her there like that with her big jugs
heavin up and down and the sweat runnin off her forehead. Maybe
the smell of the place too; fishy and damp and musty. And the dark
of the room, little cracks of sunlight through the walls. I dont know,
I got excited. I picked up the handle of a gaff and held it to her face.
She made a run and tried to get around me but I just shoved her
down on top of the nets. I had a bit of height on her. She looked

back and forth from the gaff handle to me bloody head to the fresher blood drippin off me hand. She lay back on the nets then. And dont think I wasnt quick about it either. She never made no fuss, just lay there lookin at the wall. I got blood all over the side of her face but she never made a peep.

Couple of days later I seen her going into her house. I went up and knocked on the door but she wouldnt come out. I s'pose where she was a couple of years older she didnt want no one getting the wrong idea. Shag her anyhow I said, say nothing saw wood.

'Bout a year after that I started knockin around with Margie Cahill. She was never with no one before me though. And of course I never let on about me and Teresa Bennett. Far as Margie was concerned, her first time was a first for me too. Still, at the time, I felt a bit cheated by the whole Teresa thing. And, to be honest, when she was tossed outta that truck down in Bay Bulls that time and cracked her neck and the whole Shore was gettin on about what a lovely girl she was and how she never said boo, well I'd just have a glance in the mirror and I'd see this little scar in the corner of my eye and I remembers thinkin, well everything comes back to haunt you. She got hers, just like everyone else. Yeah, I remembers thinkin that way alright.

Judge said if I'da been a year older he'd love nothing more than to lock me up for good. Life-seven. Like they were doing me a favour. Even after they screwed it up. And me lawyer, Mr. Legal Aid, he never once opened his mouth to argue. They all had me pegged. Angus, up on the stand with his nose drippin and the sweat streamin down his face, sayin there wasnt no money, none that he was aware of. No sir. Lies.

And the night I was on the run, the night the purse was found, I had something naggin at me, some loose end I couldnt gather up. Me jeans and shirt and socks and even me drawers I'd tossed over the stage head. But something wasnt right. And it never came to me till eight weeks later, the day she walked into the courtroom with her new blue dress on. The necklace with the little watch. I'd forgot all about it. Mr. Prosecution took it out of a plastic bag and held it up. My mother's necklace. And Margie said where she got it and who gave it to her. And she pointed me out, like I was some kinda dog that mighta bit her when she was a youngster. And she sat awful close to Harold too, that day.

But then of course when what's-her-face, that old bag from down the harbour that claimed to be Mrs. Alfreda's oldest friend, Rita Boland, took the stand to identify the necklace, she couldnt. At least not beyond a shadow of a doubt, as they says. All she could say was that it was "very similar" to one she'd seen Mrs. Alfreda wearin almost twenty years before. But I knew where the necklace come from, and that it was never worn around Mrs. Alfreda's neck. Mr. Legal Aid just sat there and nodded, lookin at his own watch every now and then. Never made a peep, when anyone could tell her statement was useless. Sure I was the only one *in* to Mrs. Alfreda's place in years. No one else hardly spoke to her around town; most crossed the road when they seen her comin.

But when Poppy's guts were actin up or the cow was calvin, who was the first to be called on? And now she was gone and suddenly they're all her nearest and dearest.

Old Rita proved a bit useful that day though, if only to clear up something for me.

She told how Mrs. Alfreda kept her flag at half-mast for near on forty years cause of the way her husband died. Tied a rope around his neck and jumped down an old well. Missin for nearly a week before she found him. How they'd lost their daughter in the undertow off Claire's Head two years before and he got awful low-minded. Child's name was Claire. Husband's name was Jude.

The jacket was what really screwed me. How stunned was I? I shoulda tossed it off the stage-head with the rest of me stuff.

But it was me leather jacket. They took it off me when they locked me up. Then I got word that it'd been marked as evidence. I'd wiped it down. But they had this stuff to spray on the leather and they found ahh… *indeterminate* type of blood on me sleeve. Indeterminate. That was the word. I'd no clue what it meant at the time. Figured out later that it just meant they had no way of knowin whose blood it was, not for sure. Mr. Legal Aid, snorin into his chest. I hadda elbow him to wake up.

Shoulda pled guilty all the same. Cause when you're guilty and you says you're not, when you tries to fight it, well you can find all kinds of ways to make yourself believe your own lie. And that can drive you cracked after a while. Seven years.

Harold, the prick, identified it as my jacket.

"People of the jury you will note that the witness has confirmed that the leather coat is the property of the defendant, Mr. Traynor."

And then they dismissed him. Harold. He looked right lost for a minute, like he thought he'd be needed for more. He glanced at me when he was leavin. He wasnt long lookin away.

And of course some old fella from Cape Broyle testified he saw me passin in front of his house at about two o'clock on the morning of the fire, and an old one from Witless Bay said she saw me walkin in front of *her* house an hour later. So none of that made any sense, if you knows the lay of the land. But I had to sit through it, stunned, arse-foremost slop like that.

    No, it wasnt the truth that sent me away. Never the truth. Sure, the fire started at three, and where was I then, by one account? Walkin through Witless Bay.

Jesus. That was some blaze. I watched from me bedroom window, the glow of it over the trees. Crossed me mind to go up and help out when the crowd started gettin around, but I stank like kerosene.

    Ambulance. Fire truck. Big commotion till about daylight. I stepped out on the back porch when I seen Don Keough passin down our lane. He broke the news to me, gentle as he could, that poor old Mrs. Alfreda must have knocked over a lamp. Put his hand on me shoulder then. Nodded. Like he was tryna say sorry, cause he knew how I was friendly with the old girl.

    And… I went to sleep then. I dont remember *feelin* too much about any of it, at the time.

After I got out of Dorchester I went west. Cause how could I come home really? Toronto. Sudbury. Fucken Calgary. Finally I washed up in B.C. Cash job clearin brush for a logging company. I was crashin with these lads in an old house in Port Alberni. No rent or nothing. One weekend, right outta nowhere, it struck me. All of it. Boom. Floored me. What I went and done. When I was only seventeen years old.

One of the b'ys, this dirty hippy type, says to me:

— What's your story anyway Traynor?

It all struck me. I couldnt talk, like me mouth just wouldnt work. I wanted to blurt the works of it out, that I used to be someone else, that some other part of me went and did... that. But I couldnt say nothing. Next few weeks, out in the bush in the sun, black flies eatin me alive, it was all I could think about.

Got word about Angus in the Waterford. And I think sometime in there it started runnin around in me head that maybe it was time to get home.

I went off the head when I hit a certain age. Mrs. Alfreda didnt like the states I'd show up in. One night she smelled liquor off me and another night she caught me rootin around in her upstairs bedroom. She never told me not to come back. I just didnt, much.

Quit school for good when I turned fifteen. Cut tongues. Sold some gear for Angus. Came to the point where I realized I had me own say over what I done with me own time, and that the cost of going against someone else's orders isnt that high after all. Scatter

nailin. Didnt have to listen to the nuns another second. Turned me desk bottom up. Mounties? Go to Hell. And if I wanted to spend me money on draws and booze, then Mrs. Alfreda really had no say in the matter. Not like she owned me or nothing. Only one I didnt square off with was Angus. He'd see me dead if his temper pushed him that way. Granted, we got on better once he saw I could be some use to him. But he was gettin more and more shagged up by the day. Everybody was always out to get him, out to rip him off. I learned to step around him, like I said.

And Margie. Of course. She occupied me. It was through her I found out.

Margie's crowd is from further up the Shore. Fermeuse. Her father was some ticket. Gary Cahill. A real boozer. He'd only one arm. Blew the other one off with his own shotgun. Yanked it by the barrel through a wire fence. Trigger hooked in the fence post. Boom. Crawled home. Arm hangin by a bit of flesh. Took to the bottle for good. First night Margie brought me home he batted a big tin ashtray at me with the arm he had left. He said:

— You're Angus Traynor's b'y are ya. You lost?

And I said no I wasnt lost and I wasnt Angus's. And he said yes you are. And before I could argue any further Margie pulled me through the house so's she could show me her bedroom.

Later on that night I could still hear him, down there at the table, his glass clinkin and the radio down low. I got up and went down to him. He slid his bottle towards me. I went to the cupboard for a glass.

He was slurrin. I asked him what he knew about me father.

Gary Cahill knew Len from the boats.

The *Lady Margaret* ran aground off Cape Race in the fog. Full load. Leonard J., kicked off in his bunk. Bunks were about fourteen feet long so's two men could lie down, foot to foot. In the middle there's a steel support beam, a pole. Len sound asleep when the boat struck. He drives forward in his bunk, hard, his two legs spannin the pole. Crushed hisself. They were takin on water. He couldnt walk, couldnt stand up, couldnt stop screamin. Cook struck Len with a cast iron pot. Loaded him into the lifeboat like that. Len woke up in the hospital in St. John's. He was married to my mother then, going on three years. So when the time come to show the world a youngster, so said Gary Cahill that night, well, Len hadda find some way to save face.

— And didnt Angus jump at the chance young Traynor? Your mother was a fine piece of skin.

I flew at 'im then, one arm or not, no difference to me. I had 'im around the throat and pinned to the floor and the whole house come runnin down to the kitchen. One of Margie's brothers hauled me off of 'im, smacked me in the mouth, and then I was out on the road waitin for Margie to bring me me boots.

Angus Traynor. Uncle Angus.

Soon's I got back down the Shore I dug out that old flask Mrs. Alfreda gave me. *Traynor, Leonard J., First Mate.* I brought it down to the Head, gripped the flask like you would a skimmer rock and let drive with it out into the black water. Barely even made no splash.

Started sellin for Angus more regular around when I turned sixteen. Dope and shine. Mushrooms. All up and down the Shore people had either a grin or a grievance when they seen me comin.

Some wicked nights fried on the shrooms.

Me and Harold done 'em once and I spent the whole night talkin him out of bawlin, tryna keep him from crackin his head off the road. Margie tried one time with me. Christ, it was good. Just talkin. Great big ideas she had, about, I dont know, how to fix what's wrong in the world. What keeps us breathin, she'd say. And I'd go, well cause your heart's beatin. And she'd say yes but why does your heart keep beatin? Retarded stuff like that that had nothing to do with nothing.

One evening I done 'em on me own though and I was in a bad way, comin down. I made it back to the Cove just when it was comin on dark. Couldnt face the house, so I wandered down around Claire's Head and tried to straighten up. The Head is part of Mrs. Alfreda's land, so I wasnt too surprised to see her come down through the woods. She stopped when she seen me and I thought for a second she was gonna go the other way. But she didnt. I couldnt help smilin at her. Never seen her with a cane before.

I said hello. She looked me up and down. She knew I was stoned.

— What are you puttin that old garbage into yourself for Jude?

— I knows who me father is.

She looked at me good and hard then, right through me, like the little scrap I was when she first took me home, like I knew and understood nothing. And maybe that was pretty handy to the truth. I hadda look away. We stared out over the Head. There was a swell on and I'd say a bit of an undertow. We never spoke for a while. I let her break the quiet.

— Better you hears it from me Jude, 'fore some drunk down the harbour tells ya their own version.

They fought over *me*, Len and Angus. The night I was born. And Shannon, me mother. They fought over her. Wasnt no big secret. My mother was from up Chance Cove, came down around our way in the summers. Len, mad for Shannon from day one. Had a bit of a scare. Married quick. False alarm. They tried for a couple of years after to have a child, Alfreda said. Then the *Lady Margaret* went down, and when it finally sunk in that they wouldnt be havin no family, well they all sat down and had the big discussion. For the sake of a greater good, she said.

Give your wife over to another man. Your own brother? It took a couple of months see, for her to get pregnant. I s'pose that's where it all got a bit twisted.

— Your mother was a good lookin woman, Jude. And Angus was a fine man, back then, believe it or not.

She spat into the wind. I felt me ears clickin when I swallowed.

It was agreed that Len would pay Angus for his… service. Make it easier on hisself I s'pose. Twenty dollars every time. That's a lot of money back then. But Angus'd hand the money straight over to Shannon, me mother. And me mother'd hand it on to Mrs. Alfreda for safe-keepin, I s'pose. She told me she could count that money today and tell me how many times Angus and my mother lay down and tried. Then, when me mother finally got pregnant Len cut 'em off, wouldnt let Angus come around, wouldnt let Shannon alone with him. And the racket started.

Angus musta got it mixed up in his head along the way, thought that he was in it for good, that he'd share the child, share me, and maybe even father the next one when it was wanted. But Len only needed the one. And the night I was born they fought like dogs while my mother lay dyin on the daybed and Alfreda was cleanin me up. She said Angus wanted to take me. That he almost cried when he saw me. But when Len saw me he just shook his head. He saw Angus's son, not his own.

Mrs. Alfreda stood a little closer to me then, rubbed her hand through me hair. I wanted to pull away, but after a few seconds it felt right nice anyhow.

— But Len wasnt about to let Angus have ya Jude.

And they fought. Out in the front yard in the snowstorm. Len with Angus facedown in the snowdrift, pummelin the back of his skull, knuckles full of his brother's blood. Mrs. Alfreda had to go out with the broom and crack it down on Len's back to get him off Angus.

Len musta only realized then and there that Angus'd actually *been* with my mother. Mustve all struck 'im the once. Wouldnt know but Angus'd done it behind his back. And maybe my mother actually liked Angus? Maybe she preferred him. Who knows? Anyhow, by the time they knocked off fightin, me mother was dead. And Angus lay there in the snow, bawlin for her. Alfreda said that's the last she seen of 'im. He was never the same man after. All for the greater good. Here stands that greater good they were all bankin on.

I was stoned. I had nothing to say.

She said how Len spent the first couple of years afterwards in a haze. So she reared me up for a while. She even hadda name me. And then one day Len snapped out of it and him and Angus went and got that boat. The *Shannon Marie*. She said she remembers the first time she seen the name blazoned onto it down at the wharf. How she knew there was nothing good gonna come of it. But they made a go of it for a couple of seasons. Then one evening she stood on the Head watchin 'em at the gillnets. Claire's Head is the best little nook in the harbour for a gillnet. No good for a trap though. Len was back on to Angus and they looked to be arguing. Couldnt make out the words but she's pretty sure she heard my name on the wind.

Len turns and strikes Angus, hard, knocks 'im down in the hole of the boat. Len turns back to the nets, like nothing happened. Angus flies back at 'im, bounces up outta that hole and clocks Len on back of the skull with the boathook. Len falls forward. Angus reaches out to catch him, latches onto the hood of Len's oilskin, but it rips free from the rest of the jacket. Len goes face-first into the black. Straight under. But, she said, Angus stayed out till well after dark, steamin back and forth, callin out to Len, his brother, till he lost his voice. Pokin at the water with the boathook.

Claire's Head, whatever way the rocks are underneath, when the tide hits a certain way and the wind is up, it's like a vacuum down there. Len wasnt comin back up. And Angus howled for him. She said it bounced off the cliffs from the Head to the South Side. I s'pose a brother must be something special, no matter what kinda history you got with him.

She laid her hand on me shoulder and gave it a squeeze.

I wish I coulda put me arm around her then. If I did have the chance to go back you know, that's prob'ly the point I'd pick. If I could change one thing, I'd go to her, right there in that moment and just, I dont know, give her a little hug.

I asked her why she never done nothing, never told no one.

— Say nothing, saw wood, she said her own father used to say. You're better off lettin people have their lives and carry their own burdens in their own way.

I ran then. Tearin mad again, down through the woods and onto the path towards the cliffs. I was Angus's son. And that's all I'd ever be. Mounties, smirkin down their noses at me that night when

I told 'em me father was dead. Years of sideward looks and whispers and how I got the notion sometimes that people were being too nice to me.

I was always Angus's son.

I went down around the cliffs, stoned like that, wrecked. Stumblin blind into the trees, barely clingin on sometimes to the side of the bank. The rocks jagged and angry twenty feet below. The pitch-black harbour there. Mockin me. Leonard J's bones still tumblin somewhere in the tides.

I thought about jumpin, me arms outspread and me eyes closed tight. Jump. No comin back. Body bashed to pieces on the rocks. Sucked under and devoured by the cold and the pull of the tide.

But I stayed there perched on the edge of the cliff. Shiver. Bawl. Snot. That scummy rusty mushroom taste. Leonard J. Uncle Angus. Shannon Marie. Mrs. Alfreda. Gary Cahill. Teresa Bennett. Lawlor. All the rest of 'em.

I had to get out. St. John's, the Mainland. Far away is where I needed to be.

It was the fall of the year and everything was dyin.

I coulda left that morning, got out on the highway, stuck me thumb out and disappeared. No goodbyes. No tokens of peace. Vanish.

But I talked meself into waitin. Stick it out for one more winter. Gather up a bit of money. Wait for the warm weather. I dont know. I s'pose I wasnt ready to go. The very prospect of leavin, the notion that I could, well I let that be enough.

Bitter cold all that winter. Never saw much of Margie, 'cept the odd Saturday night. Mike's Hotel in Cape Broyle opened up a snack bar in January. Fish and chips and hamburgers and chicken. Me and Angus lived on it. It got to be alright too, me and him, shagged up and sullied as he was all the time.

I never went back around Mrs. Alfreda's no more.

Angus asked about her still.

— Check in on the old bag lately? We should go up some night and rob her blind. Some money she got.

And I laughed at that. But he never.

— She used a fucken scissors Judy. If your mother hadda gone to the hospital with you she'd still be alive today.

I couldnt tell him what I knew. That was a line I couldnt cross with him. He wasnt able to talk like that. I mean, what would he have done or said? Things woulda changed for us I s'pose? Father and son united? Not likely.

Three days I waited, after the fire. Nothing, not a word of a robbery or anything out of sorts at all. I helped dig the grave. Angus was there, cursin the cold. The ground was hard as a rock and all hands were going on about what a sin it was for an old woman to go like that, that she shoulda went in her sleep, in peace.

That was generally the talk around town.

I waited for three days before I went back to the stable. That's where I'd stashed the purse with the envelope. One hundred and sixty dollars. That's what Len paid to Angus. Eight times Angus lay with me mother. Or at least eight times he was paid for it. I remember countin that money out and knowin I could never use it, never spend it. If I hadda just tossed it or buried it or burnt it.

The night of the fire, hours before, I was down in Witless Bay to a dance. I had a load of gear with me belonged to Angus. About an ounce of hash and a good four hundred bucks worth of mushrooms and even some acid. Angus said he needed to get rid of it, that he needed the money fast. He was up on bust, thought the Mounties were watchin the place, watchin him. He thought everybody was watchin him. He kept going over to our kitchen window and peekin down towards the road while he spoke. He was wired. Paranoid.

I was plannin on sellin the hash in dimes and grams, as usual.

But Angus had me lined up to unload the other stuff in one go to a couple of arseholes from the Goulds. I nodded at him, no big deal. He flew across the kitchen at me, grabbed me by the throat and pinned me to the far wall. He pressed a greasy old spatula under me top lip, sliced me gum open. First time he laid a hand on me in a long while.

— Fuck this up and dont show your face here no more. I'll cleave it off ya.

And I saw it in his eyes, cold and more bloodshot than blue and full of some new desperation and not so far from murder. He meant it. He'd kill me. He would kill me.

I thumbed down the Shore and waited outside the dance hall for Margie. But the bus was late. Harold was there, droolin over some young one from Mobile. I asked him to hang around while I made the deal with the arseholes from the Goulds, but he was too cold, wanted to go inside. Harold. Sure enough then, the second he went in to the dance the lads from the Goulds showed up.

I was stupid about it all.

They were older, in their early twenties.

Mounties were after being around earlier so we went out behind the hall. I was playin the Man, that's where I fucked meself. The big man with the dope. And I no sooner had it out of me pocket when I felt the first dart in the face, straight in the nose. I went down. I made a grab for a leg. Big shitstorm of boots and fists. I said something about Angus. They all started laughin. I passed out. Time I came to, the music from the hall was stopped and the bus was blowin the horn. I couldnt hardly move. Dont know how much time passed. Then I heard someone shoutin me name and footsteps crunchin on the ice. I opened me eyes. Beatle boots. Harold. He helped me to me feet and wiped up me face with his scarf. He tried to drag me around the side of the building but I had trouble with the legs and he had trouble with the boots. We cut the corner just as the bus was pullin out of the parking lot.

Another dream I useta have, in jail, us catchin up to the bus and the driver pullin out, over and over, just when you'd think he was gonna open the door there'd be the big rev of the engine and she'd take off into the night.

If the bus just hadda stopped.

Harold had a bit of a flask left. I drained that. Stomped around the parkin lot. Had a smoke. I was cracked. I couldnt hardly breathe through me nose and I wanted to kill anyone who even looked like they might have cousins in the Goulds. I got out on the road and started thumbin that way. But Harold got on the other side with his thumb out and when a car stopped for him I ran and got in too. That was some close. If I'da got a run the other way and never went back up the Shore that night?

A fella from Kingman's owned the car. He'd later testify to that. When we came to the crossroads in the Cove and Harold told him to stop, buddy turned around and asked me if I wanted to go any further. And where I never seen Margie first nor last I almost said yes, I'll go as far as Fermeuse. I almost did say that.

But we got out. Me and Harold. Long trek down to the North Side and we knew it wasnt likely there'd be a car, so Harold slunk off into his grandmother's place. He told me I was allowed to come in too, that I was welcome. But I walked down into the dark on me own. And I was just climbin the hill on the North Side when I slipped me hand in me inside pocket and remembered, shit, I had nothing for Angus. No dope, not a cent to me name. The Goulds arseholes cleaned me out. Close on five hundred bucks worth, all told. He'd have me head. No way I was talkin me way out of it, the state he was in when I left him. He'd kill me. He would kill me. I stood on the road lookin across the harbour, wonderin what to do. Maybe turn back, sleep it off at Harold's grandmother's after all. I dont know.

Never managed to save a penny all winter long. Still plannin to skip town when the weather warmed up. April maybe. To think that I just hung around that extra few months so Angus could put an end to me. I didnt know what to do.

And then the hatbox. The necklace. That envelope. Money in her purse too, prob'ly. Something I could hand over to Angus to at least soften the blows. Anything. Slip in and out through the back. She slept good and solid. I'd risk it. I had no hard feelings or nothing towards her. None. I mighta told meself afterwards that I did. Like how she'd messed everything up and my mother died. Sliced my mother's belly open with a scissors. How she had my mother's necklace hid away and she'd no right to it. It was mine. That's how I got thinkin, later. That's how me head twisted it up, so I'd just lie there in me bunk imagining what I could have been thinkin at the time. But like I said, I wasnt thinkin none of them things.

I followed the old horse track through the woods in back of her house. Long time since I'd laid eyes on Sal. I waited outside her back door for about ten minutes before I went in. Just get in and out and deny it when the time comes. A good wind. I almost changed me mind. But in I went. I was dead sober. Careful. I wasnt drunk at all. I remember thinkin I was, really believin it too, when I was questioned about it. Because I figured I must have been.

I went in through to the kitchen. The stove was roarin. I stood still and listened. Nothing. The wind. Stood up on the wood box, opened the cupboard above the stove. The old hatbox. Stepped down, brought it over to the table. Opened it. The necklace, right on top. Held it up, let it sway back and forth in me hand. Then, from closer than I expected:

—Who's there?

She's there on the daybed. She never sleeps on the daybed. She makes a point of climbin the stairs every night.

—Who's there?

I stands still, not even breathin. The heat from the stove.

— Is that you Jude?

I dont answer. She gets up and hobbles towards me.

— Jude my love, what happened to your face…?

She sees the hatbox, the necklace in me hand. She grips me by the forearm. The strength in her hand. I pushes at her. She's in her bare feet and reaches out for the stove to balance herself. Her free hand flat on the cast iron damper. The screech out of her. She wont let go of me arm. I'm tryna pull it free. The grip she got. I pushes at her again and again. She wont stop sayin me name and I… I hears Angus, in me head:

— If your mother hadda gone to the hospital with you, she'd still be alive today.

Grabs up the poker from the ash bucket, swings it at her. She screams. Loud. I strikes her down, keep her from makin so much racket. She hits her head off the corner of the stove. She aint down for good. It's… I'm… I've no intentions of hurtin her. Not in any way. It just. Happens. Once it starts I cant go back. Not that I'm afraid of what she'll say. It's just, I dont know, it's for her own good. I'm helpin her somehow. Mrs. Alfreda. Raise the poker. Glance up into the corner of the room. There's that old fox. She'd stuffed him, mounted him on a junk of birch. His mouth was never right, sunk in a bit on the left. His eyes two little black mirrors. In the fox's eyes I sees Mrs. Alfreda, lyin there with her arm stretched into the air, reachin out to me to help her. I almost do. I wants to. Cant turn back. Her sewing kit in the rocking chair. Pair of blackened steel scissors stickin out. Grab 'em. Feels right. Takes her by the hand, jabs the scissors into her armpit. She grunts. It wont do the job. Glance at the fox. The certainty of his death when I struck him.

Here, you'll have to tap him with this…

Pulls the scissors out and drives it into where I figures her heart must be. The steel breakin through her breastbone. Grindin roughness. Sand under your feet. Pulls the scissors out. Something lets go inside her with a small pop.

And you can see it, you can. In her eyes. That light. She's gone.

I knows it sounds ugly, but it's like my body done it all, my hands, like I was useless to save her. Came a point when I figured I was doing good by her, to kill her quick.

I never said a word, the whole while. I never once spoke to her.

Rifled through the hatbox. Found the envelope. Her purse was on the table. I snatched it, stuffed the envelope in and went for the door. Then I turned back. She wasnt movin. She was dead. Blood pooled on the floor. All over me clothes. Can of kerosene in the pantry she kept for the lamps. I poured it all around the kitchen. Soaked the bookshelves, drenched her in it. Shook the last of it at the fox. Lit the match and watched the flames. Then I ran. I looked back once to see the flames bustin out of her front window. Caught fast. That battered old flag flappin at half-mast. The heat on me face.

When the flag caught, I had to force meself to turn away.

— There's always someone dead or dyin somewhere, Jude.

I dug out a pair of lined coveralls in our old stable. Stashed the purse in the manger underneath the hay. Went through the house and stripped outta me clothes, they were soaked in kerosene, wonder I never went up in flames too. Blood. I bundled the clothes into a canvas bag with a rock, took the bag down to the stage head and tossed 'em into the water. I was like some kind of robot, not thinkin, just movin. Couldnt bring meself to toss the leather jacket, like I said. I went back to the house and scrubbed. And scrubbed. And scrubbed. Kerosene and blood.

Angus conked out on the daybed in the front room, the whole while.

Sirens.

Daylight.

Don Keough's hand on me shoulder.

I went back in and lay down. Slept the sleep of the dead.

Once they figured out there was robbery involved, she was exhumed. I never heard that till after I was arrested. They dug her up. Poor woman. I was sittin in the lockup with a robbery charge when they come around and bumped it up to non-capital murder.

In the days after the fire Angus never once mentioned the dope he'd sent me off with. I waited for him to make a roar at me, but he didnt. He probably couldnt even remember givin it to me that night. Not a word about the state of me face. And then all the ruckus with the fire and the graveyard. He never touched a drop all that week. I wanted to take off some bad though, get outta town. I kept sayin, tomorrow, tomorrow Jude. Go up and get the purse tomorrow. But I knew I wouldnt be able to touch it, not if it was stuffed with all the money in the world.

Angus found the purse. Or Sal did. A week after Mrs. Alfreda was buried. Angus went out to drive old Sal away from our stable. Sal's big thick head pushin at the side wall, the doorway gone lopsided. Angus drilled a rum bottle at him. Sal would have knocked the stable down that day. And he had the purse in his mouth. Dropped it at Angus's feet and took off runnin up through the woods again. I saw it all from me bedroom window. Angus turnin the purse over and over in his hands. He took the envelope out. That old money. Leonard's money. His money. My mother's money. He knew. I watched him slip it into his pocket, the envelope. He looked up towards me window then and I met his eye. We stood there like that.

Said he had to go to the Mounties. Said he'd give me an hour. I mean, all he had to do was toss it in the stove, the purse. And no one'd ever be the wiser. I told him I didnt know nothing, that I never done nothing.

— Just go Jude b'y. Just go.

Angus now. Believe that? Angus turned me in. He didnt have to. Think him of all people shoulda been able to make sense of what I was after gettin meself into. I scrambled to get a bag packed. He was sittin at the kitchen table when I came downstairs. Just sittin there, not movin. Starin at the floor. I stood there with me bag.

Me jacket slung over me shoulder. After a long while he said:
— Why?
Couldnt tell if he was talkin to me or not, so I never answered him.

~ ~ ~

I dont know.
Why.
There was an undertow.
Seventeen years old.
Never leave the prong lyin flat in the hay.
Great Saint Jude.
Lost causes.
What else can I say?
Nothing.
Saw Wood.

Acknowledgments

Percy T., Sherry White, Lois Brown, Donna Francis, Amy House, Ruth Lawrence, Marnie Parsons, Resource Centre for the Arts, Jenny Rockett, Janet Russell, Gerry Squires, SummerWorks Theatre Festival, Sheila Sullivan, Charlie Tomlinson, Agnes Walsh, Des Walsh, Newfoundland and Labrador Arts Council.

Originally written as a novella, *Say Nothing Saw Wood* was adapted for the stage; the script received one of the Government of Newfoundland and Labrador's Arts and Letters Award in 2005. The play enjoyed a sold-out run at St. John's LSPU Hall in 2007; it was revived in 2009 for the SummerWorks Theatre Fest in Toronto, where it won the Contra Guys Award for best dramatic script. It has since been remounted in Newfoundland and Labrador by actor Darren Ivany. Another version appeared on *EarLits 1*, an audio anthology of short fiction from Rattling Books.

    This little book is not the stage play. It's a short novel, a long short story: it's the original text from which the play was adapted.

Pen and ink drawings by Gerald L. Squires are from the Ferryland Downs, an on-going series, and are copyright the artist. They appear with his kind permission.

ISBN 9780986611391

The type is Adobe Garamond; the papers are Cougar Vellum Text
and the cover Strathmore Ultimate White Wove.
Graphic design by Veselina Tomova of Vis-à-Vis Graphics of St. John's, NL;
printing by The Lowe-Martin Group of Ottawa, Ontario.

Running the Goat
Books & Broadsides
Cove Road
Tors Cove, NL A0A 4A0